To Dez, Wren, and Sterling. Pass it on.

Ace Landers

To my wife and best friend, Marybeth

Garrett Taylor

Editorial by **Eric Geron**

Design by **Winnie Ho**

Materials and characters from the movie *Cars* 3. Copyright © 2017 Disney Enterprises, Inc., and Pixar. All rights reserved.

Disney/Pixar elements © Disney/Pixar; rights in underlying vehicles are the property of the following third parties: Hudson, Hudson Hornet, Nash Ambassador, and Plymouth Superbird are trademarks of FCA US LLC; Dodge®, Jeep® and the Jeep® grille design are registered trademarks of FCA US LLC; FIAT is a trademark of FCA Group Marketing S.p.A.; Mercury is a trademark of Ford Motor Company; Chevrolet and Chevrolet Impala are trademarks of General Motors; Mack is a trademark of Mack Trucks, Inc.; PETERBILT and PACCAR trademarks licensed by PACCAR Inc., Bellevue, Washington, U.S.A.; Petty marks used by permission of Petty Marketing LLC; Carrera and Porsche are trademarks of Porsche; Sarge's rank insignia design used with the approval of the U.S. Army; Volkswagen trademarks, design patents and copyrights are used with the approval of the owner, Volkswagen AG; Background inspired by the Cadillac Ranch by Ant Farm (Lord, Michels and Marquez) © 1974.

Published by Disney Press, an imprint of Disney Book Group. No part of this book may be reproduced or transmitted in any form or by any means, electronic or mechanical, including photocopying, recording, or by any information storage and retrieval system, without written permission from the publisher. For information address Disney Press, 1101 Flower Street, Glendale, California 91201.

Printed in the United States of America

First Hardcover Edition, April 2017

10 9 8 7 6 5 4 3 2 1

FAC-034274-17048

ISBN 978-1-4847-8127-2 (Trade edition)

ISBN 978-1-368-00908-9 (Barnes and Noble edition)

Library of Congress Control Number: 2016958413

Visit www.disneybooks.com

LEAD THE WAY

By **Ace Landers**

Illustrated by **Garrett Taylor**

Inspired by the film

Disney PRESS

LOS ANGELES · NEW YORK

YOU always need SOMEBODY IMPORTANT in your life, SOMEBODY WHO . . .

STAYS BY YOUR SIDE

and teaches you . . .

to show up and
WORK HARD.

Somebody who reminds you that when you can't do something right the **FIRST** time . . .

KEEP PRACTICING.

YOU'LL GET IT EVENTUALLY!

And somebody who points out that when
you make a mistake, it's up to **YOU** to

SMOOTH IT OVER...

even when there's a long road ahead.

You need that important somebody to show you that even when **YOU THINK YOU KNOW IT ALL,**

there's always SOMETHING
MORE TO LEARN.

SOMEBODY who teaches you . . .

that being **A TRUE**

CHAMPION

doesn't always mean winning . . .

and reminds you to **THANK THOSE WHO HELPED YOU SUCCEED.**

You need that **DRIVING FORCE** of a **SOMEBODY** to demonstrate that when you're **UP AGAINST A WALL**, there's always

A CREATIVE WAY

to turn things around.

That's what an **IMPORTANT SOMEBODY**...

shows you on and off the track.

WHO KNOWS?

Maybe one day down the road you will find **SOMEONE** looking to **YOU** for guidance . . .

and you will have **SO MUCH TO SHARE.**

You will help that someone

FACE FEARS...

and **BELIEVE**
IN THE IMPOSSIBLE.

You will inspire that **SOMEONE** . . .

to **GIVE BACK** to others . . .

and you will show that someone how to

SHIFT GEARS

and have fun!

You will be there to
CROSS THE **FINISH** LINE
WITH THAT SOMEONE . . .

and prove that the trophy **ISN'T** the only reward. . . .

The **TRUE REWARDS** are the FRIENDS and MEMORIES you make along the way.